Words to Know Bef ___ ___ ___ d

beautiful

coach

colorful

flower

garden

pollen

practice

stage

sunflower

umpire

www.rourkeeducationalmedia.com

Edited by Precious McKenzie
Illustrated by Robin Koontz
Art Direction and Page Layout by Renee Brady

Library of Congress PCN Data

Run... It's a Bee! / Robin Koontz
ISBN 978-1-61810-200-3 (hard cover) (alk. paper)
ISBN 978-1-61810-333-8 (soft cover)
Library of Congress Control Number: 2012936801

Rourke Educational Media
Printed in China, Artwood Press Limited,
  Shenzhen, China

rourkeeducationalmedia.com

customerservice@rourkeeducationalmedia.com   •   PO Box 643328 Vero Beach, Florida 32964

Run... It's a Bee!

Written and Illustrated
by Robin Koontz

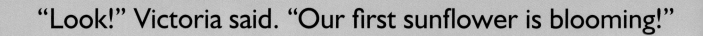

"Look!" Victoria said. "Our first sunflower is blooming!"

"I can't see it," cried Jasper.

"I'll pick you up so you can see it," said Benjamin. Benjamin lifted Jasper. Jasper stuck his nose into the sunflower.

Yellow pollen stuck to Jasper's nose. "What a beautiful sunflower!" said Jasper.

"Buzz! Buzz!" said a bee.

"Run…it's a bee!" Jasper cried.
They ran from the garden as fast as they could.
Jasper bounced on Benjamin's shoulders.

The bee chased after them.

The bee zipped and zoomed as they raced across the playground. They ran into a baseball game.

"Everybody run!" Jasper cried. The runners on the bases ran home. They thought that someone had hit a home run.

"FOUL!" cried their coach.

"They are all OUT!" cried the umpire.

All the players ran after Victoria, Benjamin, and Jasper as they dashed towards the school. They raced through a door and onto the school stage.

The bee buzzed and zoomed behind them.

An actor was holding some colorful, fake flowers. "Run…it's a bee!" Jasper cried. All of the actors started running.

The bee swirled around the fake flowers.
Then it circled over Jasper's head.

Victoria, Benjamin, Jasper, the baseball players, and the actors all charged down the hall. They bolted out the door.

"Buzz! Buzz!" The bee followed them.

14

"Look," said Victoria. "There's our garden!"
Everyone stopped at the garden fence.
Benjamin put Jasper on the ground.

"Where did the bee go?" Jasper asked.

"Buzz! Buzz!" said a bee.

They watched as the bee landed on Jasper's nose.
The bee gathered the pollen with her feet.

16

"Hum!" said the bee. She flew back to the sunflower.

"What were you so afraid of?" asked one baseball player. "The bee just wanted the pollen that was on your nose."

"I guess so," said Jasper.

"She didn't sting you, did she?" asked Benjamin.

"No," said Jasper. "I guess we were running for no reason!"

"Those are beautiful flowers," said one of the actors. "May we have some for our play?"

19

"Yes, you may!" said Victoria, Benjamin, and Jasper. "You can practice your play right here!"

Everyone enjoyed the play, including the bee.

After Reading Activities

You and the Story...

What time of year do you think the story takes place?

Why did the bee chase Jasper?

Have you ever been stung by a bee?

Words You Know Now...

Two of the words from the list below are used to describe something. Write them on a piece of paper. Now use them to write a sentence that describes two other words on the list.

beautiful
coach
colorful
flower
garden

pollen
practice
stage
sunflower
umpire

You Could...Find Out More About Bees!

- Go to the library or use the Internet. Look up bees.

- Where do bees store the pollen?

- What do bees do that is good for flowers?

- How do bees make honey?

- Present your findings in a poster or model to your classmates.

About the Author and Illustrator

Robin Koontz loves to write and illustrate stories that make kids laugh. Robin lives with her husband and various critters in the Coast Range mountains of western Oregon. She shares her office space with Jeep the dog, who gives her most of her ideas.

Ask The Author!
www.rem4students.com